WHO IS MAY AND JASMINE'S NEW NEIGHBOR?

Jasmine walked close to the barn where Joey's pony used to live. For a moment she thought she could almost hear Crazy nickering and stomping in the stable. Then she listened more carefully. There was definitely something in the stable. Maybe the new neighbor had horses. That would be great!

"Aaah-ooooooooow!"

A loud wail cut through the twilight.

Jasmine took off, running all the way to May's stable.

"You heard it, too?" May asked before Jasmine had a chance to say anything.

Jasmine nodded. She was out of breath. She was also too scared to talk. . . .

Pony Crazy

BONNIE BRYANT

Illustrated by Marcy Ramsey

A SKYLARK BOOK
NEW YORK • TORONTO • LONDON • SYDNEY • AUCKLAND

RL3 007–010
PONY CRAZY
A Skylark Book / July 1995

Skylark Books is a registered trademark of Bantam Books,
a division of Bantam Doubleday Dell Publishing Group, Inc.
Registered in U.S. Patent and Trademark Office and elsewhere.
Pony Tails is a trademark of Bonnie Bryant Hiller.

ISBN 0-553-48255-6

Published simultaneously in the United States and Canada

Bantam Books are published by Bantam Books, a division of Bantam
Doubleday Dell Publishing Group, Inc. Its trademark, consisting of the
words "Bantam Books" and the portrayal of a rooster, is Registered in U.S.
Patent and Trademark Office and in other countries. Marca Registrada.
Bantam Books, 1540 Broadway, New York, New York 10036.

PRINTED IN THE UNITED STATES OF AMERICA

O   0 9 8 7 6 5 4 3 2

Pony Crazy

Pony Crazy

1 Saying Good-bye

Jasmine James jumped up and down with excitement. "Go for it, May!" she yelled.

May Grover heard Jasmine shout. She could also hear the pounding hooves of Jackie Rogers's pony. Jackie had almost caught up with her. May leaned forward in her saddle.

"Come on, boy," she said to Macaroni. Her pony's yellow mane fluttered in the wind. He was going as fast as he knew how. Then, somehow, he sped up. They pulled ahead. May was going to win!

Her teammates were waiting for her at the end of the ring. They were leaping and waving at her. May was the final rider for the relay race and she had the red flag in her

1

hand. All she had to do was get across the line.

May stayed low in the saddle. She gripped the reins tightly. She held on to Macaroni with her legs. She stared straight ahead at the finish line. With a final burst of speed she crossed it. She'd won!

"Yippee!" Jasmine yelled. She reached up and gave May a hug. Then she patted Macaroni on his neck. "If we can do this well in practice, just think how great we'll be in the real race next week!"

May shook her head. "By the time we have the real race, Joey won't be here," she reminded her friend.

The two girls looked at the boy who stood next to them. Joey Dutton just stared at the ground.

"It's not your fault that your family is moving," Jasmine said softly.

May, Joey, and Jasmine lived next door to each other. Joey lived in between May and Jasmine. They had been neighbors since they were born eight years before. But that wasn't all they had in common. They each had a pony that they kept in a stable in their backyard. Now all that was going to change.

Pony Tails

Joey's parents had sold their house. They were moving.

Joey and the girls had been dreading this day. Now here it was. While the three of them were riding their ponies, Joey's parents were helping movers load up a van. Dr. Dutton was coming to pick up Joey and his pony, Crazy, in a little while. Then they'd both be gone.

Joey was only moving two towns away, but things would never be the same. His pony wouldn't be in the backyard between May's and Jasmine's houses. And he wouldn't be at the Pony Club meeting every Saturday.

The three riders all belonged to a Pony Club called Horse Wise. Horse Wise met at Pine Hollow, a stable in Willow Creek, Virginia. Now Joey would have to join a new Pony Club—Cross County Pony Club.

May and Jasmine didn't like to think about Joey being gone.

Joey looked up at his friends. "Don't worry," he said. "There's no way I'll be able to beat you two in a relay race when I'm at Cross County."

"I'm not so sure about that," said May. "Who knows who Max will put on our team after you move?"

Max Regnery was their Pony Club instruc-

Pony Crazy

tor. He owned Pine Hollow and made his riders work very hard. He didn't care if they won their competitions. He said the important thing was for his riders to do their best. May still thought riders did their best when they won.

Now Max was trying to get everyone's attention. "Horse Wise, come to order!" he called out. "This was a good practice. We're going to do well against Cross County Pony Club in two weeks. Because Joey is leaving, I'll make up new teams and let you know what they are. That's all for now. It's time to untack your horses and ponies."

Untacking meant removing saddles and bridles. May, Jasmine, and Joey were good at that because they owned their own ponies and knew what to do.

Today they finished quickly. Then the two girls tied up their ponies and walked with Joey and Crazy to the driveway. His father, Dr. Dutton, was there, waiting with the horse van.

May could feel her eyes stinging. She turned away from Joey so he wouldn't see the tears. Instead of saying good-bye to Joey, she said good-bye to Crazy. She gave him a carrot. Jasmine gave the pony a hug.

Then Joey led Crazy up the ramp onto the van. He snapped the door shut.

"I'm going to miss you guys," Joey said.

"We'll miss you, too," said Jasmine. "Come visit us."

Joey nodded. He looked as if he wanted to cry, too.

"Time to go," said Dr. Dutton to Joey. Then he said good-bye to May and Jasmine. "Don't look so sad," he said. "Wait until you meet your new neighbor. She's *very* interesting."

"Bye," said Joey. He got into the front seat next to his father and waved.

"Bye," called out Jasmine and May as the van pulled away.

The van drove away. May swallowed hard. That was the last time Joey Dutton would be their neighbor. She knew Jasmine felt just as sad as she did. They stood there together until the van disappeared down the dusty road.

"What do you think Dr. Dutton meant when he said our new neighbor was interesting?" Jasmine asked as they headed back to the stable.

"Interesting usually means different," said May. "When my mother says dinner is interesting, she means it didn't come out right." She stopped and looked at Jasmine. "I hate to tell you this. But I think Dr. Dutton was trying to tell us that our new neighbor is strange!"

2 May and Jasmine

When May and Jasmine went back into the stable, Outlaw tugged at his lead. He was Jasmine's pony and he was ready to get going. He knew he'd have fresh hay and water as soon as he got home.

"Don't worry, boy. We'll be home soon," Jasmine said. Outlaw sniffed curiously at her pocket, looking for a treat.

Outlaw was a solid brown color called liver chestnut. He had a white face that looked like a mask, which was why Jasmine had named him Outlaw. He was a Welsh pony with a long mane. He could be frisky. He could even be temperamental. May said he and Jasmine were a perfect combination because they were so different from each other.

Jasmine thought May and Macaroni were a

perfect match, too. Macaroni was a sweet pony. He never nipped at May and he always did exactly what she told him to do. He was the color of May's favorite food—macaroni and cheese, which was how he'd gotten his name.

The girls collected their ponies and headed back down the driveway.

"I hope Dad gets here soon," said May. "Last time he picked us up, he was an hour late."

"That was because your sister Ellie had soccer practice," Jasmine reminded her.

"It was because she got into trouble in soccer practice and had to stay late," May said. May had two older sisters, Ellie and Dottie. Neither of them loved ponies the way she did. She couldn't understand how *anyone* could not love ponies. Her mother loved them. So did her father. Her father trained horses for a living, so the stable in their backyard always had lots of horses and ponies in it.

Jasmine didn't have any brothers or sisters. She lived alone with her parents. Although May said being an only child would be nice, Jasmine liked being around May's family. They were loud and rowdy and always seemed to be having fun, even when they were arguing. There were always lots of people around. Mr. Grover's work was in the stable in the backyard—and in the riding ring attached to it—so he was always at home. While he worked, he had a radio blasting out old rock music so he could sing along.

Jasmine's house was very quiet. Her father worked for an environmental group, which meant his job was to help protect the planet. Her mother was an artist. She had a studio in their house and while she worked, her radio played chamber music.

May and Jasmine's personalities were just as different as their families. May was stubborn; Jasmine was gentle. Jasmine liked to dress up; May liked to wear jeans best. May was always in a hurry; Jasmine was patient. Jasmine finished her homework as soon as she got home from school. May finished it just before she went to bed—sometimes later if her mother didn't notice her light was on.

The two girls also looked very different from one another. Jasmine was taller than May and thinner. She had long wavy blond hair and blue eyes. She liked to wear her hair in braids or in a ponytail. She always looked neat and tidy. May had very straight brown hair and brown eyes. When she wore a

Pony Crazy

ponytail, her hair would straggle out of the ribbon. She had a ski-jump nose and in the summertime it was covered with freckles.

Even though they didn't look alike or act alike, the girls were best friends with one big thing in common. They both loved ponies more than anything in the world. In fact, they were totally pony crazy.

May and Jasmine both heard Mr. Grover honk at the same time. He was driving a station wagon, which pulled a van for the horses. He hopped out of the car and went to open the van for Macaroni and Outlaw.

"Hi, girls," he greeted them cheerfully. Then he noticed their sad faces. "What's wrong?"

"Joey's gone," they said at the same time.

That made both girls so sad that they couldn't even do what they usually did when they said the same thing at the same time: Give each other a high five, a low five, and then say "Jake!"

Today, without Joey on their team or living next door, there was nothing to laugh about.

3 May Gets Suspicious

At home May led Macaroni into her family's stable. They were greeted there by Mrs. Grover's bay gelding.

"Hi, Dobbin," May said to the horse. Dobbin had the first stall in the stable because he was the most curious. He put his head over the stall door every time he heard a sound. He kept it there until he found out what had made the sound.

May patted his soft nose with her left hand. Macaroni sniffed at Dobbin. Dobbin sniffed at Macaroni.

"Hello, Rascal," May said to her father's horse. Rascal winked at May and Macaroni as they passed.

"Nice to see you, Hank," she said to the gray horse in the next stall. "And greetings,

Vanilla," she said to the Thoroughbred in the stall across from Hank. Vanilla belonged to one of her father's customers. He was staying at the Grovers' for a few months while Mr. Grover trained him.

"Dad says that one day you're going to be a great jumper," May told the beautiful horse. "I'll be able to say I knew you when you were just a beginner!"

Vanilla eyed her suspiciously. Vanilla often looked suspicious. Her father had told May not to touch Vanilla because he was very temperamental. He could even be dangerous. It was hard to think of such a pretty horse being dangerous. But May had seen him rear once when her father was riding him. Her father had almost been thrown off the horse's back. May wouldn't want to be anywhere near Vanilla when he was that upset. She waved at the horse and walked on by.

May groomed Macaroni in his stall and gave him fresh hay and water. Then she gave him a final pat and left, saying good-bye to Vanilla, Hank, Rascal, and Dobbin as well. She didn't want to leave anybody out.

On her way back to the house, she couldn't help looking over at Joey's house. It was completely empty.

Pony Tails

I wonder if Joey likes his new house, May thought. His old room had looked out on his old stable. She hoped he had a window that looked out onto his new backyard stable. That way he could see Crazy whenever he wanted.

May glanced up at the window that had been Joey's. It was dark. Empty. Or was it?

May blinked. Then she blinked again. Had she seen something moving in the house?

There it was again. A light flashed on—then off. It did it again, this time for longer. That's strange, thought May. It almost seemed like a signal. But who would be sending a signal? And to whom?

Then May remembered what Dr. Dutton had said about the new neighbor. He'd said she was strange.

No, May reminded herself a second later. He'd said she was "interesting." She and Jasmine had decided that "interesting" meant strange.

May stood watching in the twilight. But the house seemed empty again and completely dark. May shrugged and continued on toward her own house.

Just as she reached the back door, she heard the sound for the first time. It was a shriek. It was a howl. It was both. And it was coming from the Duttons' house!

May didn't wait around to find out what had made the noise. Instead she ran as fast as she could. And she didn't stop running until she was inside, upstairs, with her bedroom door shut tightly behind her.

4 The Moving Van

May took a deep breath. "There are no such things as monsters," she told herself.

Then she listened carefully. There were no strange sounds coming from outside. All she could hear were her sisters Ellie and Dottie arguing. Mrs. Grover was telling them to stop it.

May let out her breath.

"Aaah-ooooooooow!" came a sound from outside her window.

May gasped. She crouched behind her bed. She was scared but also curious. She wanted to know what was making the sounds and what was flashing the lights on and off.

She crept around the end of her bed and crawled all the way to the window. Then she heard tires screech. She stood up to see out-

side. There was no car screeching its tires. There were no cars in the street at all.

But parked outside the Duttons' old house was a great big truck from Frank Stein's Moving and Storage. The side door was open and there was a ramp leading to the ground. On the front of the van, it said WE MOVE ANYTHING!

Two men came out of the house. In the streetlight May could see that their shirts read STEIN'S. They must be the moving men, thought May.

She watched as they took a couch into the house, then came out again a moment later.

"Let's get the big one," said one of the men.

The *big* one? May wondered.

They disappeared into the truck.

When they returned, they were carrying a cage. It was a big cage.

May tried to think. It was too big for a hamster or a bird. It seemed too big for a cat or a dog. It was big enough to hold a . . .

"Aaah-oooooooooow!" came the sound again.

A monster?

May dropped to the floor.

No way. There were no such things as monsters. Monsters only existed in movies and books, not in real life.

Pony Crazy

She made herself look out the window again. Now the men were carrying a great big stainless steel table into the house. And a big machine with dials, lights, tubes, and arms.

That's the kind of stuff a crazy scientist uses for weird experiments, May thought.

Was this Dr. Dutton's idea of an "interesting" neighbor?

May looked again at the moving van. This time she noticed the sign on the side of the truck.

FRANK N. STEIN'S MOVING & STORAGE. Frank *N.* Stein? That sounded just like Frankenstein!

"Oh my gosh," May said out loud. "Wait till I tell Jasmine about this!"

5 Jasmine Hears Something

Jasmine blew on the final spot of paint. She was finally finished with her diorama for school. It was called "Women at Work." It showed women working in the United States Congress.

Jasmine stood a doll in front of the diorama. She had made a navy blue suit for the doll so it would look like a Congresswoman.

It's perfect, she thought happily. She hoped her teacher would think so, too. But as Jasmine admired her work, the doll's head tilted to the right. Jasmine frowned. She straightened it out. Then the doll's head tilted to the left. Oh no, she thought. Maybe this won't work after all.

She heard a buzz. It was her walkie-talkie. May was calling her.

Pony Crazy

"Hi, May," she said. "What's up?"

"We have to meet," her friend replied.

"I'm in the middle of—" Jasmine began.

"Right now!" said May.

Jasmine was surprised by the sharp sound of May's voice. It must be something important, she thought.

"Where?"

"Macaroni's stall." Then May clicked off the walkie-talkie. She was gone.

Jasmine put the doll down. She could fix its head later. Her friend needed her now.

Jasmine told her mother she was going over to May's, and hurried out the back door. The girls always crossed through the Duttons' yard to get to one another's houses. Jasmine was almost halfway to the Duttons' stable when she remembered it wasn't the Duttons' house anymore.

At least it's dark out, she thought. Maybe no one will notice me.

Jasmine walked close to the barn where Joey's pony used to live. For a moment she thought she could almost hear Crazy nickering and stomping in the stable. Then she listened more carefully. There was definitely something in the stable. Maybe the new neighbor had horses. That would be great!

"Aaah-ooooooooow!"

A loud wail cut through the twilight.

Jasmine took off for the Grovers' stable, running all the way to Macaroni's stall. She was glad to see that May was already there. She didn't want to be alone.

"You heard it, too?" May asked before Jasmine had a chance to say anything.

Jasmine nodded. She was out of breath. She was also too scared to talk. She sat down next to May outside Macaroni's stall. Both girls liked the Grovers' barn. It always felt safe.

"I heard tires screeching, but there was no car," said May.

"I heard a terrible howl," said Jasmine.

May nodded, her eyes opened wide. "I think a mad scientist moved in next door," she said.

Jasmine stared at her friend. Sometimes May exaggerated. Sometimes she jumped to conclusions. Sometimes she had wild ideas. And sometimes, she was right.

May told Jasmine all the things she'd seen carried into the house.

"Maybe it's just somebody weird like the cat lady on Granite Street," Jasmine said.

Pony Crazy

"Remember her? She had forty-three cats living in her house."

"That wasn't a cat I heard," said May.

"Me neither." Jasmine sighed and rested her chin on her knees.

"And the cat lady didn't have strange tables and weird machines," May reminded Jasmine.

"There must be some explanation," Jasmine said.

They heard a thumping sound. But it was a nice, familiar sound. It was the sound of a horse's hooves entering the barn.

"Hi, girls!" said Mr. Grover. He was leading Vanilla to his stall.

"Hi, Dad," said May.

"Hello, Mr. Grover," said Jasmine.

Mr. Grover closed the door of Vanilla's stall and reached over to pat Macaroni. The pony liked to be patted. Then Mr. Grover looked over the door to Macaroni's stall.

"May, did you notice anything wrong with Macaroni's right front leg? It looks like he's got a sore foot."

May scrambled to her feet and looked into the stall with her father. Something *was* wrong. Macaroni was holding up his right foot so only the tip of his hoof touched the floor of the stall.

"I'll check it," she said. "Maybe I missed a stone in his shoe."

May went into the stall. She picked up Macaroni's right front foot. She felt under his shoe with her finger. There didn't seem to be anything there. She put the foot down.

"Check his lower leg," said her father.

She ran her hand down Macaroni's right leg, holding it gently. Then she felt his left leg. The right one was definitely larger.

"It's swollen," she said to her father.

"I thought so," he said. Then he came into the stall with May and felt Macaroni's leg himself. "What do you think we should do?" he asked.

May thought hard. There were a lot of things that could make a horse lame. Some of them were serious. Some of them weren't. Sometimes an owner could tell and sometimes a vet was needed.

"I think Judy should check him out," she said. Judy Barker was their vet.

"I think you're right," said her father. "What should you do in the meantime?"

"I should put a bandage on the leg. That will protect it from getting worse," she told him. "It will give him extra support, too. No riding until we know what it is."

"Very good!" said her father. "You're really learning a lot at Horse Wise, aren't you?"

"Max makes us work hard," said Jasmine.

"Max is a good instructor," said Mr. Grover.

He handed May a long cloth bandage. She began wrapping it around her pony's leg.

May heard a familiar click and then a hissing sound. It was the intercom that connected the Grovers' house to the barn.

"Jasmine? Are you there?" Mrs. Grover asked.

"Yes, Mrs. Grover," Jasmine called toward the box on the wall.

"Your mother's on the phone. Your dinner's ready!"

"Please tell her I'll be right there," said Jasmine.

"Okay," Mrs. Grover replied over the intercom.

Jasmine stood up. "I'd better go. Good luck with Macaroni."

"See you tomorrow," called May. She went back to wrapping the bandage around Macaroni's leg.

"Not too tight," said her father.

Pony Tails

May nodded and concentrated very hard.

Jasmine started walking home quickly. From outside the Grovers' barn she could still hear May talking to her pony.

"Hold still, Macaroni," May said.

Jasmine smiled to herself. Macaroni was good at holding still. He would behave for May. Jasmine thought about how much trouble Outlaw gave her when she tried to wrap his legs. He never stood still.

Suddenly her stomach rumbled. Jasmine realized she was very hungry. Luckily her mother was making vegetable lasagna, her favorite dinner.

Then her stomach made a louder noise. At least that's what Jasmine thought until she heard the sound again.

It wasn't her stomach—it was a cackle! It was loud and it sounded mean, like a witch. Someone—or *something*—was laughing, and the sound was coming out of the Duttons' house!

6 Jasmine Gets Some Help

Everything was quiet at the Duttons' house on Monday morning. Jasmine didn't hear any howls or cackles. There were no lights flashing on and off. Jasmine wondered if she and May had made it all up. She didn't think so.

At 7:45, she left her house to wait for the school bus. It wasn't easy because she was carrying her congressional diorama as well as her backpack and lunch box. She also had to carry the doll in one hand. The doll was going to look bad enough with a lopsided head. Jasmine didn't want to mess up her hair, too.

As she walked up to the bus stop, Jasmine looked around for May. She wanted to ask May about Macaroni's leg. She also wanted to know if May had heard any more sounds coming from the Duttons'.

But May wasn't at the bus stop. Jasmine looked down the street past the Duttons' to May's house. Judy Barker's truck was in the driveway. That explained it. The vet must be looking at Macaroni's leg. Someone would drive May to school a little later. That meant Jasmine would have to wait to get her questions answered. And she'd have to carry the diorama all by herself.

When Jasmine reached the bus stop, Wil McNally pointed to her diorama. "What's that?" he demanded.

"It's an assignment," Jasmine told him. She turned away. She didn't even like to talk to him. Wil McNally was a big bully. He was always teasing people and picking fights. The last thing she needed today was Wil making fun of her.

When the bus arrived, Jasmine carried everything onto the bus. The driver helped her by holding the diorama until she was up the stairs. Then Jasmine took it to an empty seat. She put the diorama on the aisle seat next to her and held the doll carefully on her lap.

Wil was behind her. He stopped when he got to her seat. He looked at her. He looked at the diorama. There was a gleam in his beady brown eyes. He didn't say anything. He just sat down—right on her diorama!

"Get off that!" Jasmine shrieked.

"It's only an assignment." Wil grinned.

The driver stood up and started walking over. Wil quickly moved to another seat.

The cardboard was bent and wrinkled. Weeks of work were ruined! Jasmine swallowed hard. She wasn't going to let Wil McNally have the satisfaction of seeing her cry.

For the rest of the trip, Jasmine sat still and stared straight ahead. When they got to school, she waited so that she'd be the last one off the bus. She didn't want anyone else to wrinkle or bend the diorama.

As soon as she was on the sidewalk, Jasmine stopped to examine the damage. The diorama now had a bulge in one wall and a dent in another.

I'm going to kill Wil McNally, she thought.

She picked up the diorama in one hand and her lunch box and the doll in the other. Suddenly the doll's head rolled along the sloping sidewalk in front of the school. Jasmine dropped the diorama and her lunch and chased after the head. She stopped it with one foot—as if it were a soccer ball.

Jasmine groaned. Nothing was going right and school hadn't even started yet. Then the bell rang. She had two minutes to get to her classroom. Along with everything else, she was going to be late!

She couldn't hold back the tears now. They started rolling down her cheeks.

"Do you need some help?" someone asked.

Jasmine turned to see a girl she'd never seen before. She was wearing a bright blue jacket—just like one Jasmine used to have—and she had a nice smile.

Jasmine smiled weakly in return. "Only if you know how to fix dolls' heads."

The girl in the blue jacket picked up the head, and took the doll's body from Jasmine. She looked at both parts.

"Hmmm," she said. She turned the doll's body so she could see better. "I wonder . . ." She turned the doll's head so she could see inside it better. Then she poked inside the doll's body. "I have an idea."

"You do?" Jasmine asked.

The girl nodded, reached into her backpack and pulled out a tool. It was something Jasmine had seen many, many times. It was a hoofpick—the tool that was used to clean horses' hooves.

Pony Crazy

"Do you ride?" Jasmine asked.

"Sometimes," answered the girl in the blue jacket.

"I ride, too," Jasmine began. "My friend and I . . ." She let her words trail off. The other girl was concentrating very hard. Jasmine knew she shouldn't interrupt.

The girl in the blue jacket stuck the hoofpick into the doll's body. Then she tugged. Something moved, but Jasmine didn't know what it was. Next, the girl stuck the hoofpick into the doll's head. It took two tries. Jasmine couldn't see what she was doing, but she held the hoofpick steady when the girl told her to.

"There!" the girl in the blue jacket announced. She gave Jasmine the doll. Its head was back where it belonged, and it was on straight.

"Wow! You did it!" Jasmine handed the girl her hoofpick.

"Yeah, I did, didn't I?" the girl said proudly. There was a big smile on her face. She put the hoofpick in her backpack.

"Thank you!" Jasmine said.

The bell rang again. Now they were both late. The hall monitor stood at the front door of the school. She waved angrily at the girls. "Time to get to class, girls!"

Pony Crazy

"We better hurry," Jasmine said.

"Right," agreed the other girl. She rushed into the school building, brushing her straight black hair back from her face. Jasmine grabbed her slightly wrinkled diorama, her perfectly repaired doll, and her lunch. She ran after the girl in the blue jacket.

When she entered the school, there was no sign of the girl or her blue jacket.

As Jasmine hurried to her classroom she decided she'd try to find the girl later. She wanted to thank her again and find out her name.

7 Macaroni Needs a Hand

The minute she got home from school that afternoon, May went to the barn. As she hurried to Macaroni, she greeted the other horses. "Hi, Dobbin; hello, Rascal. Hey, Hank." Vanilla was in the back of his stall stomping angrily. She didn't say anything to him. Macaroni was waiting for her.

She patted and hugged him. He nuzzled her shirt pocket, looking for a carrot. She gave him one.

"Okay," she said. "Time to look at your leg."

That morning, Judy, the vet, had said that Macaroni's injury wasn't serious. So far May had done everything right. His leg needed to be wrapped in a bandage and he should only have light exercise. That meant May couldn't ride him until the swelling was gone.

May knew that things like this sometimes happened to horses. Owners had to be patient with them or the horses would only get sicker. May was not very good at waiting for most things, but with Macaroni, she could always be patient. Especially since Judy had promised that his leg would be all better for the mounted games against Cross County Pony Club. That was what May was most worried about.

She unwrapped Macaroni's leg and felt for swelling. It was still swollen. She rewrapped the leg. "Time for a walk," she told him.

May looked at the paddock behind the stable. She could let Macaroni out in the paddock, but there was no telling what a loose pony might do. He might run around. That would be too much exercise. Or he might stand completely still. That wouldn't be enough exercise.

The only way to be sure to do the right thing was to walk with him, as if he were a dog.

That's a great idea, thought May. I'll take Macaroni out on a lead, just the way people walk their dogs.

She clipped a lead line on the pony's halter and led him out of the stable. She waved to her father, who was riding Vanilla in the training ring. He waved back.

"Come on, boy," she said. Macaroni followed. She took him out of the barn and through the backyard. She passed by the kitchen door where her mother was baking something that smelled delicious. She walked out into the street in front of her house.

May and Jasmine lived on a quiet country road. There were no sidewalks and only a few cars passed by. Elm and maple trees grew along the side of the road, shading the street. It was a nice place to take a horse for a walk.

May glanced over at the Duttons' house. She didn't see anything strange. She didn't hear anything strange. That was good. Still, May didn't want to take any chances, especially when she had to take care of Macaroni. She turned right, away from the Duttons' house.

Macaroni followed May. His shoes made a nice clip-clop sound as they struck the road. She listened carefully. The clips and the clops were even. That was good because it meant that Macaroni wasn't favoring his sore leg.

Pony Crazy

Macaroni paused to sniff at grass and leaves near the McNallys' house while they walked. He lifted his head suddenly. He'd heard something.

May looked where her pony was looking. She groaned. It was Wil McNally!

Wil was in his front yard. He was playing with his dog, a big greyhound named Dave. When May passed his house, Wil stopped and stared at them. His jaw dropped as if he'd never seen such a sight as a girl walking a horse.

May looked straight ahead. Maybe if she pretended not to notice Wil, he wouldn't say anything mean. She and Macaroni walked on.

Wil went back to playing with Dave.

May sighed with relief.

The houses were far apart after the McNallys'. The land became more hilly and covered with trees. It was a state forest, filled with trails and paths where May and Jasmine liked to ride. So did Macaroni. His ears perked up and he sniffed eagerly.

"Not today," May told him. "We can't ride into the woods on the trails. We have to walk by the road so you can have your light exercise. That way we'll be able to have all the fun we want when you're better. Maybe Mom will let Jasmine and me go on a picnic on Sunday. Would you like that?"

Macaroni snorted. May decided that was a definite yes. May gave him a hug.

"Is that your boyfriend?"

May turned around. Wil McNally had stopped playing with Dave. Now he was following May and Macaroni on his bike.

"No, it's my *pony*," May retorted. "And he's nicer than any boy in the whole town. Smarter, too!"

Wil smirked. "If he's so wonderful, how come you have to walk him like a dog?"

"He's got a sore leg," May shot back. The minute she said that she was sorry.

Wil never missed a chance to tease her.

"It's probably from carrying you," he said.

May glared at him. She decided not to say anything else.

"That must be why his sock is all wrinkly, too." Wil laughed.

May looked down at Macaroni's leg wrap. It *was* wrinkled.

Oh no, she thought. May knew from practicing in Horse Wise that a wrinkled leg wrap was worse than no leg wrap at all. She had to fix it, but she didn't want to do it in front of

Pony Crazy

Wil. She didn't want to give him the satisfaction of knowing he'd found her mistake.

She had to get rid of him. Her mind raced. Then she got an idea.

She shaded her eyes with her hand and looked back down the road. "Was that your dog?"

"Huh?" Wil said.

"Running after that squirrel, I mean," May went on.

Wil looked where May had been looking. There was no sign of his dog, Dave. There was no sign of a squirrel, either. But Dave was a very fast runner and liked chasing squirrels a lot. Wil had to find out. He stepped on the pedal of his bicycle, turned around, and headed in the direction May had pointed.

May sighed with relief. Now he'd leave her alone—at least until he got back to his house and found Dave still in the yard.

She knelt down and removed the bandage from her pony's leg.

"I'm sorry, Macaroni," she said. "I didn't do a very good job, did I?"

Macaroni stood patiently while May tried to reroll the bandage. It had to be rolled up smoothly before she could put it back on the pony's leg. May sighed with impatience. Wil would be back any second, and May wasn't very good at rolling bandages. She was on her third try when she heard bicycle wheels behind her.

"I think I hear your mother calling you, Wil," May said without looking up. "She says your rich aunt Sylvia just arrived. Isn't she the one who brings you good presents? You'd better hurry!"

"Are you all right?" a voice asked. It wasn't Wil's voice.

May turned around then to see who had spoken. It wasn't Wil.

It was a girl about her own age. She had straight black hair which she wore short with bangs cut across her forehead. That was just the way May wanted to have her hair cut, but her mother liked it long.

May's face turned red. "I thought you were someone else," she said.

"I know. I don't have a rich aunt Sylvia—but I wish I did!" The girl with the black hair laughed. She had a nice laugh and a nice smile. May laughed, too.

"What's the problem?" the girl asked May. She pointed to the pile of unwrapped bandage.

"I'm not very good at leg wrapping and

Macaroni needs a bandage. It was all wrin-kled."

"I can give you a hand." The girl climbed off her bike and set down the kickstand.

To May's surprise, the girl rolled up the bandage quickly. A few minutes after that, she'd bandaged the leg with a smooth, snug wrap.

"Nice!" May declared. This girl knew a lot about taking care of horses. "Thank you, too."

"You're welcome," said the black-haired girl. "I've got to go now."

With that, she climbed back onto her bike, zipped up her blue jacket and was off, riding down the road. "See you!" she called over her shoulder.

May waved after her. She didn't know where the girl had come from or where she was going. But she was glad she'd been there.

May tugged on Macaroni's lead. The horse stepped forward comfortably. The tighter bandaging job was just what he needed.

May felt bad. She'd never even asked the girl her name. But she was sure she'd see her again. She'd know her right away by her nice smile and laugh—and especially by that great haircut.

8 The Night Visitor

A little while later, Macaroni was back in his stall and May was in her room, working on her math homework. She opened the book to page 73 and saw 100 problems. Yuck, thought May, I'll be doing math problems all night!

May picked up her pencil, but instead of starting the homework, she picked up the walkie-talkie and signaled to her best friend.

"Hi, May," Jasmine answered right away.

"How did everybody like your diorama?" May asked.

"It was really good—especially because I met a girl in a blue jacket who fixed the doll's head. Remember the blue jacket I used to have—my favorite one? She wore one *just* like it." Jasmine told May all about her hard morning and the girl who had come to her

43

rescue. "It was the weirdest thing. She used a hoofpick to fix the doll's head!"

"What a great idea," May said. "Who is this girl?"

"I don't know. I never saw her before," Jasmine said. "And she disappeared before I could ask her her name."

"I guess this is the day for rescues," said May. "A nice girl with the prettiest black hair helped me out. Wil McNally was being a pain as usual—"

"What's that?" Jasmine interrupted.

"What's what?" asked May.

"There's a light shining at the back door of the Duttons' house. Can you see it?"

May looked out the window of her room. It was completely dark out there. She couldn't see anything. But she heard something.

She listened. It was dogs barking. She started to tell Jasmine when she heard the weird howl again.

"Aaah-oooooooooow!"

May shut her eyes tightly.

"May!" Jasmine said. "Do you see that?"

"What?" May opened her eyes. Now the back door of the Duttons' house was open, and a tall figure of a woman in a long flowing robe stood there.

Pony Crazy

"Is it a . . . ghost?" Jasmine whispered.

Before May could answer, the figure hurried across the backyard to the stable.

"I think it's a mad scientist!" May replied. "And whoever it is is using Joey's barn as a laboratory!"

9 The New Girl

On Saturday Judy Barker came to check on Macaroni again. May waited nervously as the vet ran her hand down Macaroni's sore leg.

All the riders at Pine Hollow and Horse Wise liked Judy Barker. She loved their horses and ponies almost as much as their riders did. She also expected the owners to take responsibility for their horses, no matter how young the owners were. With Judy's help, May had learned how to check a pony's pulse and respiration before she could read. She had learned those things with her first pony, Luna. Now she had Macaroni and she was still learning.

"The leg is almost all better," Judy finally announced. "You've done a great job with him, May."

Pony Crazy

"Can I ride yet?" May asked.

"Not today," said Judy. "Tomorrow he'll be ready for a ride—a nice gentle ride. Maybe a trail ride and picnic in the woods."

May laughed. Her mother must have told Judy about the picnic she and Jasmine wanted to have. And now they could go. May couldn't wait to tell Jasmine.

*   *   *

Later that morning May hurried into the tack room at Pine Hollow. That was where the horses' saddles and bridles were stored. That was also where this week's meeting was being held. Jasmine was already there, sitting on the floor. May started to wave to her, then stopped and stared. She couldn't believe her eyes. There, standing right next to Jasmine, was the girl with the straight black hair who had helped May wrap Macaroni's leg!

"May! Come meet the girl who fixed my doll's head!" Jasmine called.

"No way!" May replied. "She's the girl who wrapped Macaroni's leg!"

"No! She's the . . ."

The girl laughed and held up her hands to quiet May and Jasmine. "I think I should introduce myself," she said. "My name is Corey Takamura and you're both right. I fixed the doll's head and wrapped the pony's leg." Then she smiled her nice smile. "I may even have another surprise for you."

Max suddenly stepped over to the girls. "I see you three have met."

"Yes, and it's a funny story, too," May began. "Wait'll we tell you—"

"Later," he said. "Right now, I wonder if you two girls could show Corey around Pine Hollow before our meeting. Then we'll put her on a pony and see how she does."

"Sure thing, Max," May said.

Pine Hollow was a stable with a lot of traditions. One of the traditions was that the old riders showed new riders the ropes. May and Jasmine were only too happy to take their new friend around.

First, they led Corey to the feed storage building.

"I should have known you'd come to Pine Hollow," May told Corey after she pointed out bags of grain. "Anyone who can wrap a pony's leg like you can just has to be in a Pony Club."

May and Jasmine showed Corey how the hay was stacked.

Pony Crazy

Corey said, "I've been riding all my life, but I've never belonged to a Pony Club. I'm crazy about riding, and I'm really crazy about my pony. And there's something else—"

"You have a pony, too?" Jasmine asked, interrupting Corey.

"Yep. His name is Samurai," she said. "But I call him Sam. Speaking of ponies, how is Macaroni's leg?"

"Much better," May answered. "This morning the vet said he's ready for an easy ride. Isn't that great, Jasmine?"

Jasmine nodded. "Outlaw will be very happy about that." Then she turned to Corey. "Outlaw is my pony. He's a liver chestnut with a white face that looks like a mask. He lives in the stable behind my house. May has a barn in her backyard, too. Where does Samurai live?"

"Well, we have a stable now," Corey said. "In fact—"

"I think we'd better hurry up." May suddenly realized the tour of Pine Hollow was taking much too long. "Let's get back to the stable and introduce you to some of Pine Hollow's ponies. They're really nice, though not as nice as Outlaw and Macaroni," she added loyally.

Pony Tails

The girls walked out of the feed storage building and back to the stable.

"I can't wait to meet Outlaw," said Corey.

"He'll be here next week for the mounted meeting and the mounted games against Cross County Pony Club. Can you play, too?" Jasmine asked.

"Sure," said Corey. "But what's a mounted meeting and what are we going to play?"

"A mounted meeting means we're on our horses at Horse Wise. Today we have an unmounted meeting. At Horse Wise, there are mounted meetings every other week," Jasmine explained.

"Mounted games means we play games on horseback. The ones we'll be playing next week are like relay races," said May.

"There's so much to learn," said Corey with a sigh.

"There sure is," Jasmine agreed. "But here comes the best part—the ponies."

May and Jasmine took Corey to the stalls where Pine Hollow's ponies lived.

"At Pine Hollow, they name the ponies after small change," Jasmine explained.

"This is Penny." May introduced Corey to a copper-colored chestnut pony. Corey patted Penny, but Penny didn't seem to notice. She was much more interested in munching on some hay.

"And here's Dime," Jasmine told her. Dime was a silver-colored pony who stayed in the corner of his stall until the girls passed by.

"He's shy," Jasmine went on.

Corey nodded, as if she understood that.

"Nickel is my favorite," said Jasmine. "He's the first pony I rode here."

"Me too," said May. Nickel was a gray pony.

"He's got the sweetest face!" Corey patted Nickel's soft nose.

"And he's the easiest pony in the world to ride," said May. "He does whatever a rider wants him to do—even if the rider forgets to tell him."

The girls went on through the stable. There was a Shetland pony named Ha'penny and a Mexican pony named Peso. Corey seemed to like every one of them. She patted them, hugged them, and talked to them just the way Jasmine and May did. One thing was very clear to Jasmine and May: Corey was just as pony crazy as they were!

"There's one more thing we need to show you," Jasmine said. "It's the good-luck horse-shoe. Whenever we have a mounted meeting, you have to touch the horseshoe before the meeting begins."

"Nobody who has ever touched the horseshoe has gotten seriously hurt," May explained. "It protects us."

"Like magic?" Corey asked.

"Exactly," said May.

"Maybe." Jasmine shrugged. "The Saddle Club says it's not magic; it's common sense. When you touch the good-luck horseshoe, it reminds you to ride safely."

"Makes sense," said Corey. "But what's The Saddle Club?"

"That's what three of the older girls here call themselves," said Jasmine. "They're best friends who are also the best riders in Horse Wise. Their names are Carole Hanson, Lisa Atwood, and Stevie Lake."

"You'll get to know them," said May. "They help us out a lot. And Max counts on them."

"Actually, Max counts on everybody," May said. "If you don't like work, you won't like riding at Pine Hollow."

Corey smiled. "I don't mind work that has to do with ponies and horses," she said.

"Good," said May. "Max makes us work so we'll learn. It also helps to keep costs down. That's good for everybody."

"Pine Hollow seems like a perfect stable," said Corey as the girls led her back to the tack room.

"Especially if you're pony crazy," Corey and May said at the same time.

Jasmine laughed. "You two have to say 'Jake.'"

May started to explain, but Corey already knew. She and May gave one another high fives and low fives, then and shouted "Jake!" together.

On their way into the tack room, May and Jasmine were thinking the same thing. Even though they'd just met Corey, it felt as if they'd known her all their lives.

"You know," Corey began, "there's something else you don't know about me—"

"Horse Wise, come to order!" Max called. Inside the tack room, the meeting was about to begin.

"We have to go in and sit down," said Jasmine. "Max hates it when riders are late to Horse Wise. Tell us later, okay?"

"Okay," Corey promised. "I will."

10 A New Teammate

Max began the Pony Club meeting by talking about the mounted games. He pulled out a sheet of paper.

"Horse Wise and Cross County will each have three teams," he said. "Not everybody will be able to ride this time. Some people will be rooting for the team."

All the riders groaned. Max held up one hand to silence everyone. "Remember, if you're not riding, you're still working for the Horse Wise team. There's plenty for everybody to do."

May sat up nervously. With Joey Dutton gone, Max might decide not to use their team.

Max looked at his paper. "The senior team will be Lisa, Carole, Stevie, and Veronica."

That made sense. They were the four best

riders at Horse Wise, even if nobody liked Veronica very much.

"The intermediate team will be Meg, April, Betsy, and Adam," said Max.

May looked at Jasmine. Would they be riding or rooting? She didn't think rooting would be nearly as much fun as riding. Jasmine looked nervous, too.

"And the junior team will be May, Jasmine, Jackie, and our newest member, Corey Takamura," Max finished.

May and Jasmine began clapping excitedly. Their new friend was going to be their teammate, too!

"Okay, okay," said Max. "Now, I know you four haven't had a chance to ride as a team. I want you to saddle up the ponies now and practice before our lunch break. Stevie, you'll help them out, won't you? The rest of us are going to talk about worming techniques."

May and Jasmine jumped to their feet. They grabbed their tack before Max could change his mind.

"Come on, Corey," May said. "You should ride Peso." She pointed to a saddle and bridle. "That's his tack. He's really fast and you'll like him."

Pony Crazy

"Okay," said Corey, picking up the equipment from the rack behind her. Her grin matched May's and Jasmine's.

May introduced Corey to Jackie Rogers and Stevie Lake. Jackie smiled warmly. Her curly brown hair bounced around her shoulders.

"Your name is Stevie?" Corey asked, looking at the older girl.

"It's really Stephanie," Stevie explained. "But the only person who calls me that is my mother when she's angry. Of course, that's hardly ever," she added quickly.

May and Jasmine laughed.

"Stevie is famous for getting into trouble," Jasmine explained to Corey.

"But I'm almost as good at getting out of it," Stevie said. "That's enough about me. Let's get to work."

Fifteen minutes later the ponies had on their saddles and bridles. The four girls were ready to ride.

They quickly mounted up. Then, one by one, they touched the good-luck horseshoe.

Stevie set up the first race. It was the flag race. She drew a line in the dirt with her boot.

"That's the starting line and the finish line," said Stevie. She looked at Corey. "Starts and stops are important in mounted games. You've got to get going fast and you've got to stop fast."

All the girls listened closely. Stevie knew what she was talking about.

Then Stevie suggested that Jasmine go first, followed by Jackie, Corey, and finally May.

Stevie stuck the flag in the ground at the far end of the ring. She took a handkerchief out of her pocket and dropped it.

The second the handkerchief hit the ground, Jasmine was off. She was riding Penny. Penny was easygoing and did everything she was told to do.

They rode down to where the flag was. Jasmine yanked it out of the ground and rode back to Jackie.

"The handoff is the most important part of the ride," said Stevie. "If the next rider isn't ready and you miss the handoff, the race is lost."

Jasmine and Jackie didn't miss. Jackie and Dime raced around the circle quickly. Then they brought the flag back to where Corey was waiting.

On the way back Dime started acting fussy. He didn't seem to want to return to the starting line. He moved over to one side. It was as if he wanted to stay away from Penny.

But Corey was ready. She watched Dime and Jackie. As Dime edged to one side, Corey nudged Peso in that direction, too. When Dime finally came across the line, Corey and Peso were right there to meet him.

Corey took the flag from Jackie. She and Peso made the trip back and forth very fast. She rode Peso back to exactly where May and Nickel were waiting. May and Nickel ran their part of the race quickly, too.

"Nice going, girls," Stevie said. She smiled at Corey. "Good job with the handoff from Jackie. If you hadn't been ready to move, the race could have been lost."

"I'm sorry about Dime," said Jackie. "He just didn't want to cooperate, I guess."

May was a little annoyed with Jackie. Ponies could be difficult sometimes, but it was the rider's job to control them. At least Corey had known what to do. It was beginning to seem that Corey *always* knew what to do.

"Let's try another race," said Jasmine.

"Okay," Stevie agreed. They tried four more races before they broke for lunch. They carried eggs back and forth on a spoon; they practiced opening and closing a paddock gate; they carried buckets of water (without spilling too much); and they shot at a target with squirt guns. They all agreed that the squirt gun race was the most fun.

"Of course it is." Stevie grinned. "I invented it!"

The riders were exhausted and happy by the time they untacked their ponies.

"You guys are a great team!" Stevie told them while she helped them with the tack. "Cross County doesn't stand a chance against you."

That was the most important thing the team wanted to hear.

"Lunch break!" Max called.

That was the second most important thing the team wanted to hear.

11 Trouble

May, Jasmine, and Corey took their sandwiches and juice to May and Jasmine's favorite place at Pine Hollow. It was a shady hill behind the stable, overlooking a paddock where horses were allowed to run free.

"Aren't they beautiful?" Jasmine asked.

"The best sight in the whole world," Corey agreed, looking at the horses. "Almost as great as watching my own pony in a field."

"I just have a small paddock area in my backyard," said Jasmine.

"I've got more space," May chimed in. "My dad's a trainer so he needs a full-size ring and a large paddock."

"We like to ride in May's paddock," said Jasmine.

"We *did*," May corrected her. "I'm not sure

we're ever going to want to ride in our back-yards anymore, though."

"Really?" said Corey. She took a bite of her peanut butter sandwich. "What happened?"

Jasmine made a face. "It's our new neighbor."

"It's creepy there now," May added.

"What do you mean?" Corey asked.

"We think some kind of weird scientist moved in," said May.

"What?" Corey stopped eating her sandwich. "How do you know?"

"There are these weird sounds coming from the house," said Jasmine.

"But maybe—" Corey started to say.

"We've heard howling and screeching," May went on. "And at night lights flicker on and off."

"You can't—" Corey began.

"May thinks the new neighbor is like Dr. Frankenstein," Jasmine added. "She might even be doing weird experiments in the stable!"

Corey's jaw dropped.

May nodded. "Wait until I tell you what we saw last night!"

"No." Corey shook her head and stood up.

May was really enjoying telling the story.

Pony Crazy

She tugged at Corey's sleeve so she'd sit down again. "We both saw it. It was the scientist—dressed like a wizard or something."

"No!" said Corey. She said it louder.

This time May looked at Corey. Something very odd was going on. Corey's face was pale. Her eyes were filled with tears. Had they scared her? They hadn't meant to.

"Uh, Corey," May began. "We didn't mean—"

But Corey spun around quickly. She ran away, down the hill and into the stable.

May turned to Jasmine. "What did we do?"

Jasmine shook her head. "We were just telling her about the mad scientist. What's wrong with that?"

"Beats me." May shrugged.

Jasmine took a sip of her juice. She thought back over the morning. "Didn't Corey say something about having another surprise for us?"

May nodded.

"I wonder what it was," Jasmine went on.

"I don't know." May stood up, looking over at the field of horses and the wide blue sky. "But I hope we have the chance to find out," she said.

12 The New Neighbor

May and Jasmine weren't happy. By the time Horse Wise was over for the day, they felt miserable about what had happened with Corey.

When Max asked them where Corey had gone, they didn't know what to say. And when Jackie asked them why Corey had run off crying, they just shook their heads. They didn't know the answer.

On the way home from Pine Hollow the two girls just stared out the window of the Grovers' car. Neither one spoke until they reached their neighborhood.

May saw it first. It was a sign outside the new neighbor's house.

"Look!" she cried, poking Jasmine.

Mrs. Grover stopped the car in front of Jas-

Pony Crazy

mine's house so she could get out. But Jasmine didn't move. Instead she stared at the sign. So did May.

The sign read GRACE TAKAMURA, DOCTOR OF VETERINARY MEDICINE.

"Takamura?" May whispered. "Isn't that like . . . ?"

"*Corey* Takamura," Jasmine said.

Mrs. Grover turned around to face the girls. "Have you met her already?" she asked. "I heard that Doc Tock—that's what everyone calls Dr. Takamura—has a daughter just your age. She has a pony, too. Isn't that great?"

Jasmine got out of the car without answering. May got out, too.

"I'm going to Jasmine's," May said. Before her mother could say no, the girls ran inside together. They were out of breath by the time they got to Jasmine's room. They dropped down on the floor.

"How many Takamura families could live in our town?" May asked.

"Who just moved into a new house," Jasmine added.

"Who live near enough to help you with a doll's head and me with a leg wrap," said May.

It was a silly question. They both knew the answer. "Just one," Jasmine said.

Finally May said the words out loud. "Corey Takamura is our new neighbor."

"She lives in between us," said Jasmine. "That's what she wanted to tell us, but we didn't let her."

"Veterinarians keep animals when they're sick," May went on.

"In big cages," added Jasmine.

"And sometimes sick animals make weird sounds," said May.

"Even scary sounds," said Jasmine.

"And veterinarians need operating tables," said May. "And big machines."

Jasmine gazed sadly at May. "I can't believe we were so dumb," she said. "We made a great new friend and now—"

"She hates us," May finished. "Our new neighbor, Corey Takamura, hates our guts. What are we going to do?"

13 Samurai

By the time May left, Jasmine still felt terrible. Corey had done something nice for each of them. All they'd done in return was hurt her feelings. How could she ever look Corey in the face again?

Jasmine stared out her window. There was the Duttons' yard, only now it wasn't the Duttons'. It was Dr. Takamura's—Doc Tock, May's mother had said.

Jasmine knew about Doc Tock. Judy Barker was the vet in Willow Creek who looked after horses. Doc Tock took care of other animals. Jasmine had just never known her name was Takamura—or that she was moving next door.

Now that Jasmine knew the truth, the Takamuras' yard looked just like the Duttons'

67

yard. The white house and big red barn were the same. There were no monsters, no mad scientists. Only a very good vet and her very nice daughter. Who probably hated May and Jasmine.

Then there was something else.

The back door of Corey's house flew open. Someone ran across the yard. It was Corey. She was going to the barn. A dog barked loudly. It was just a dog barking, not a monster.

A few minutes later, Corey came back out of the barn. This time, she was leading a pony who was all tacked up. Corey was wearing her riding clothes and riding hat.

She held her pony's reins. She patted the pony on the neck. Samurai was named for the crescent-shaped blaze on his face. It looked like a Samurai sword. Then she leaned forward and hugged the pony. Corey buried her face in her pony's mane and held it there for a long time.

Jasmine stood back in the shadows of her room. She had seen Corey's shoulders shaking. Corey wasn't just hugging her pony. She was crying, and she was crying hard. It was all their fault.

14 Practice

In a way, everything seemed normal to May. She was in Macaroni's stall, checking his leg. Her father was in the schooling ring behind the stable, working with Vanilla.

In another way, nothing was normal. May felt sick in her stomach about the terrible mistake she and Jasmine had made. How could they have hurt Corey's feelings like that? Now Corey would never be their friend again. She'd never be on their Pony Club team either.

May ran her hand down Macaroni's leg. It wasn't swollen anymore. And Macaroni didn't pull it away when she rubbed it. The leg was all healed. She could ride him now. Her mother had even said she and Jasmine could go on a picnic tomorrow. Everything

Pony Tails

would be perfect—if only they hadn't ruined their chances of being Corey Takamura's friend.

May decided to groom Macaroni. Her father always said that grooming a horse was as good for the groomer as it was for the horse. It always felt good to do something for someone else, especially when it was for her pony.

She took down her grooming bucket and set to work. Macaroni knew what was coming. He nuzzled May's neck. She hugged him back.

First she wanted to clean Macaroni's hooves. She took out the hoofpick and looked at it. That reminded her of how Corey used a hoofpick to fix Jasmine's doll.

"Grrrrrr," she told Macaroni. Macaroni twitched his ears.

She cleaned his hooves. Then she began to work with the currycomb, a brush used for cleaning horses' coats.

Macaroni stood still because he liked the attention. He even closed his eyes. May worked hard. Just as her father said, it felt good to work so hard on her pony.

Outside, May heard her father talking to

Pony Crazy

Vanilla. He said things like "Good boy" or "Nice!" or "Pay attention now." That was the way her father talked to horses. Then his voice changed. May could tell he was talking to a person now.

"Hi there," he said to someone. "Nice pony you've got there."

"Thanks," someone said back to him.

"What's his name?" Mr. Grover asked.

"Samurai" was the answer.

May's stomach flip-flopped. It was Corey. May moved to the other side of Macaroni—away from the door—so Corey couldn't see her. She still wasn't ready to face her new neighbor.

"If you sit into the saddle, the horse will stop faster," said her father.

"Like this, you mean?" Corey asked.

"Exactly. Try it from a faster gait, like a canter," he suggested.

May heard hoofbeats. They were fast at first. Then they stopped.

"Much better," said Mr. Grover.

"Thanks," Corey answered.

"You're the new neighbor, right?" Mr. Grover asked.

"Yes, sir," Corey replied.

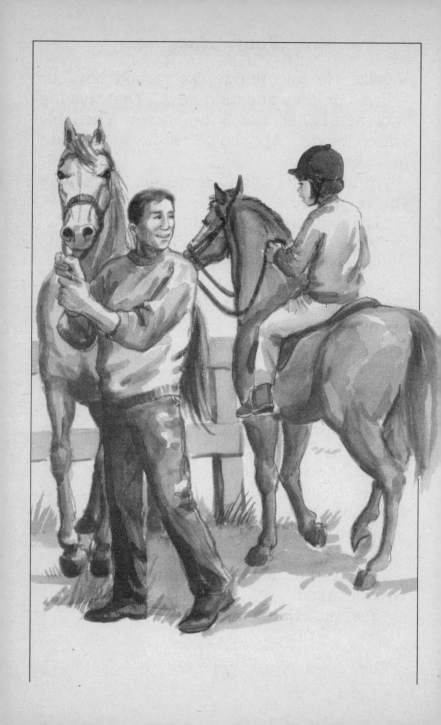

Pony Crazy

"Well, you're a very good rider. If you ever want to go out into the fields behind this barn, it's all right with me. Just don't go into any field if *this* horse is in it. Vanilla's a wild one."

"Thank you," said Corey. May thought her voice sounded a little happier. "Today I think I'll stick to the ring, though."

"Okay," said Mr. Grover.

Corey and Mr. Grover didn't talk any more. They just worked, and so did May. She combed and brushed Macaroni's coat until it gleamed.

When she was finished, she stood on her tiptoes and looked out the dingy window of Macaroni's stall.

In the small ring behind Corey's house, Corey and Samurai were working hard together. Then May realized what they were doing—working on fast starts and stops. Stevie had said that was important in mounted games. Corey must be practicing for mounted games!

Relief washed over May. If Corey was getting ready for the games, it meant that she was thinking about the good part of the Horse Wise meeting, not only the bad part.

Pony Tails

Maybe, just maybe, she and Jasmine could find a way to make up with Corey.

Tomorrow was the day of May and Jasmine's picnic. Together they would find a way to apologize to Corey.

15 The Picnic

"I've got an idea," May said as she un-wrapped her peanut butter and honey sand-wich.

Jasmine looked at her friend. "You do?"

The two girls were sitting on a big rock in the woods. Their ponies were hitched to a tree in the shade. In the distance they could see the fields and the paddocks behind their houses. Rascal and Hank were in the small paddock at the back of the Grovers' stable. Vanilla was in the field.

Jasmine took a bite of her sandwich. "So what's your idea?" she asked, almost afraid to hear the answer.

When May had ideas, sometimes they were wonderful. Like when May had a surprise birthday party for Jasmine. But sometimes

May's ideas weren't so great. Jasmine remembered the time May had decided to build a tree house in a tree that wasn't strong enough to hold it. They'd both plunged out of the tree and hit the ground hard.

"We need to help Corey with something," said May. "She helped us and now it's our turn to help her."

Jasmine nodded. "That's exactly what I was thinking."

"Let's paint the stable," May said.

"What?" Jasmine thought she'd heard wrong. This was May's idea?

"The Duttons'—I mean, the Takamuras'—stable needs to be painted."

"We can't paint a stable," Jasmine reminded her friend. "We don't know how."

"You dip brushes in paint. Then you slap the brushes on the stable," May said. "What's so hard about that?"

Jasmine had heard some pretty strange ideas from May since they'd been friends. But this was the strangest.

"May, the stable is two stories high," she said. "It's a whole barn! We can't paint that by ourselves."

May shrugged. "Okay, then, we'll just paint the door."

Pony Crazy

"What does that have to do with Corey?" Jasmine asked.

"Nothing," May admitted. "It was just an idea."

Jasmine didn't think it was a very good one.

"Could we buy her a new saddle?" May asked.

"She's got one. It's a nice one, too," said Jasmine. "Besides, we don't have enough money to buy her a saddle."

"Bad idea, huh?" May asked.

"Bad idea," Jasmine agreed.

"Then I guess we're just going to have to start digging," May said.

"Digging?" Jasmine echoed.

"A tunnel under Corey's lawn so we can get back and forth to each other's houses without crossing their lawn," May explained.

"May!" Jasmine cried. "What kind of idea is that?"

"I'm just kidding," May said glumly.

The two girls sat in silence for a few minutes. A few feet away Outlaw nickered softly and Macaroni shuffled his feet. Jasmine watched the two ponies. Sometimes it seemed as if the two ponies liked being together as much as May and Jasmine did.

A moment later Jasmine had an idea.

Pony Tails

"Maybe what we really need to do is apologize," she said softly. "Isn't that what *real* friends do?"

May looked at her and nodded. "But how?"

Jasmine shook her head. Neither of them knew the answer to that question.

Suddenly May stood up. "Look," she said. "Isn't that Corey?"

Jasmine shaded her eyes. Corey was riding Samurai in the ring behind her stable.

At first they rode in circles, walking, then trotting, and then cantering. Jasmine and May watched. They didn't say anything because they were both thinking the same thing. They were wishing Corey could be with them.

Corey worked some more on the starts and stops May's father had helped her with the day before. But her riding ring was too small for her to get going fast. She looked around, then walked Samurai out of the ring. They headed for the paddock where Dobbin and Rascal were turned out.

"May, look," said Jasmine. "Corey's going to ride in your paddock."

"That's okay. Dad told her she could," May answered.

They watched for a few more minutes. Corey was a good rider and Samurai was a good pony. It was fun to see them work together.

Then Jasmine squinted. "What's she doing now?"

"She's going into the field," said May.

At first, that seemed fine. Then May remembered about Vanilla. There was a hill halfway across the field, and Vanilla was on the other side of the hill. Corey couldn't see Vanilla, but May and Jasmine could.

When May looked at Vanilla, he was munching happily on the fresh green grass. His ears flicked up. He'd heard something. He lifted his head and sniffed. He smelled something. He pawed at the ground. He wasn't happy.

Corey couldn't see any of this. But May and Jasmine saw all of it.

"She's in trouble," May cried. At that instant, Vanilla lifted up his front feet and reared. He'd sensed that someone was invading his field—and he was going to stop them.

"Corey!" yelled May.

Corey didn't hear her.

"Corey!" yelled Jasmine.

Corey didn't hear her.

"COREYYYYYY!" the girls yelled all together. But it didn't do any good.

Pony Tails

"We should get your dad," Jasmine said.

"We don't have time," said May. "Neither does Corey!"

May looked all around. They had to do something and do it fast.

Vanilla began galloping then, climbing swiftly to the top of the hill. In a matter of seconds, he'd reach Corey and Samurai. May and Jasmine didn't want to think about what he'd do when that happened. They just had to get there in time!

16 Runaway

May and Jasmine jumped into their saddles. They unhitched the ropes from the tree branches and turned their ponies around.

Macaroni sprang into a trot and then a canter.

"Come on, boy!" May said. She used her hands and her legs to tell him that she was in a hurry.

Right away Macaroni understood. He took off, and May leaned forward. She clutched the reins; she clutched her pony's mane. She had never ridden so fast in her life.

Behind her, Outlaw's hooves pounded the ground. He was nearby and he was going almost as fast as Macaroni was.

May ducked under a branch. Macaroni swerved around a tree and jumped over a

81

rock. May stayed in the saddle. She kept her eyes straight ahead, never moving them from the field.

Then the sound came. It was a scream—Corey's scream.

"Faster, Macaroni! Faster!" May cried.

Somehow Macaroni went faster.

Now May could see the edge of the field. It was surrounded by a white fence. The gate was on the right. May turned Macaroni to the right. He followed her instructions perfectly. May opened the gate in record time and left it for Jasmine to close.

They were in the field. But where was Corey? More important, where was Vanilla?

"Help!" Corey's voice echoed over the hill-side.

May didn't even have to tell Macaroni to get going. He knew what his job was. He sprang into a gallop, racing toward the cry.

"I'm coming!" May yelled.

"Me too!" called Jasmine.

"Over here!" Corey yelled back.

The ponies circled the hillside as fast as they could, faster than Jasmine had ever thought Outlaw could gallop.

When they came around the side of the hill, Jasmine gasped. Samurai was nowhere in sight. But Corey was standing with her back to a big boulder. Vanilla was right in front of her and he was rearing.

"Vanilla!" yelled May. "Get back!"

Vanilla was startled and frightened. He flattened his ears against his head. The whites of his eyes showed. From watching her father train many horses, May knew this was a dangerous animal.

Samurai whinnied loudly then. He was running wildly along the other side of the hill.

"You get Samurai; I'll help Corey," May told Jasmine. But she didn't know how she would ever do what she said.

"Don't move, Corey. You'll frighten him more," said May.

"I can't move," Corey replied. "I don't have any place to go."

That was the truth and May knew it. Vanilla had Corey completely blocked off. The only thing to do was get Vanilla to move away.

May and Macaroni rode up behind Vanilla. "Vanilla! Here boy!" she said, hoping it would work. "Come, Vanilla!" The horse didn't move. At least he wasn't threatening Corey anymore. But Corey still couldn't get out of there.

"Come on, boy! Come here!" May called.

Pony Tails

His ears flicked toward her. May knew that meant he heard her. Then she whistled. Vanilla stood still. He turned his head to look.

She whistled again. It was working. Vanilla stepped back. Then he turned around and looked at May. She whistled a third time.

That was all it took. Vanilla whinnied loudly and reared. He'd found something new to chase. He'd decided to chase May! As soon as he moved, Corey ran to safety away from the rock. Now May was Vanilla's target.

Macaroni had spent a lot of time in the stable with Vanilla. He knew just how mean the horse could be and he knew just how fast he had to go to get away from him. May couldn't believe how rapidly her pony's short legs carried them to safety. He fled to the gate in the fence. May flung it open and they were through it before Vanilla knew where they'd gone.

Across the field Jasmine gave Outlaw a nudge. "Come on, boy, we've got to catch that pony!" Outlaw ran after Samurai. But Samurai ran like crazy.

Jasmine and Outlaw knew the field better than Samurai. They took a shortcut across the crest of the hill and moved alongside Samurai. Now Jasmine knew what to do. It was just like the flag race. She had to pick up something while her pony was moving. Only this time, what she had to pick up were Samurai's reins.

The ponies were almost neck and neck. Outlaw was gaining on Samurai. Jasmine leaned forward and reached out her right hand to grab the reins. She couldn't quite reach them. She leaned farther. Next to her, the runaway pony's hooves pounded the ground. The reins dangled near those hooves. Samurai could almost trip on them. She couldn't let that happen.

Jasmine shifted her weight forward and tried one more time. This time it worked! She had the reins.

Then, as suddenly as he had started, Samurai stopped. Jasmine slowed Outlaw to a trot. Samurai trotted right next to him. He was perfectly polite, as if he were trying to make up for running away.

"Come on, let's find Corey," she said to the pony.

She led the ponies back over the crest of the hill. Corey was standing motionless. She didn't know which way to run. Vanilla wasn't anywhere near her now, but he was watching

her. Jasmine didn't waste any time. She and the ponies rode over to Corey.

"Mount Samurai!" Jasmine cried.

Corey looked at her blankly.

"Hurry!" Jasmine said. "Vanilla will be back in a minute."

That was the last thing Corey wanted.

She took Samurai's reins from Jasmine and climbed into the saddle.

"This way," Jasmine told her. She and Outlaw began galloping to the gate. Corey and Samurai followed.

May opened the gate for them and then shut it tightly the second the two ponies and their riders were through.

The girls sat in their saddles, breathing hard and not saying anything. Then all three of them spoke at exactly the same instant.

"I'm sorry," each girl said.

Jasmine looked at May. May looked at Corey. Corey looked at Jasmine. Then they all spoke at the same time.

"Jake!" they cried, slapping their hands together.

"We didn't mean the things we said," said Jasmine. "We just didn't think."

"We were so stupid!" added May.

"And I didn't think when I went into the

field." Corey shook her head. "I almost got us all killed."

May looked again from Jasmine to Corey. "Friends?" she asked.

"And teammates!" Corey agreed. A wide smile broke out first on her face. Then it spread to May's and Jasmine's.

17 Mounted Games

Jasmine didn't take her eyes off the handkerchief. The second it hit the ground, she was off. Outlaw was being fussy, though. He didn't seem to see what the big hurry was.

"Come on!" Jasmine yelled. She pressed into Outlaw's belly with her legs.

"Get going!" May yelled. Finally Outlaw got the idea. Then he decided to make up for lost time and bolted ahead. Jasmine was so startled, she nearly fell out of the saddle.

Jasmine loved the feeling of riding a horse at any speed, but top speed was best of all. She leaned forward in the saddle and kept her eyes on the red flag.

It was like grabbing for Samurai's reins all over again. Only this time, the reins weren't moving. But Outlaw was flying!

Jasmine gripped the reins tightly in her right hand so she could grab the flag in her left. She reached out, stretching her arm. Her fingers touched the wooden pole of the flag. She grasped it and pulled. She had it! Outlaw turned obediently and raced toward home. She handed the flag off to Jackie, and Jackie and Dime took off.

Corey waited by the starting line. She couldn't cross it until Jackie gave her the flag. Then she had to get going as fast as she could. She held the reins tightly. Her legs hugged her pony's sides. She looked ready.

"Here she comes!" said May.

Corey reached out. The second Jackie passed her the flag, she gave Samurai a kick. He burst into a gallop. She stayed right in the saddle. Her ride was smooth—and fast—the whole way.

May was the last team member to go. When Corey handed her the flag, Macaroni flew across the line, racing toward the far end of the ring. "Let's go, boy!" she said. All they needed to do was win this race, and then Horse Wise would beat Cross County. It came down to this. It came down to May.

Next to her, Joey Dutton was riding Crazy

Pony Crazy

for Cross County Pony Club and he was ahead. May had to win. She leaned forward in the saddle. Macaroni started going faster. It was as if he remembered his race to get away from Vanilla. The two of them swung around and turned at the far end of the ring. It was almost over; they'd almost won.

"Come on, May! You can do it!" Jasmine bounced up and down in her saddle.

"We've got 'em beat!" shouted Jackie.

"Faster!" shouted Corey.

Macaroni went faster.

The next thing May knew, her teammates were out of their saddles, and jumping around hugging each other.

She'd won! Her team had won the race and Horse Wise had beaten Cross County.

Then all the riders and rooters from Horse Wise ran over to the junior team. Everyone was screaming and jumping with excitement.

May, Corey, and Jasmine gave each other high fives.

"Nice job, girls," Max called. He smiled proudly.

May, Jasmine, Corey, and Jackie beamed with pride. Jumping and screaming was okay, but "Nice job, girls," from Max was even better.

Pony Tails

Later that afternoon the girls were untacking their ponies.

Max came over to congratulate them again. "You girls worked hard. You have obviously all been practicing this week, right?"

May, Jasmine, and Corey each thought of the rescue in the field and how that, in a way, had helped them to get ready for the race.

"Uh . . . sort of," May said.

"Well, whatever you've done, it's worked," Max went on. "Maybe you can show the rest of the Pony Club some of the exercises you did."

They all just nodded.

"Maybe," Jasmine said. She tugged at Outlaw's saddle. It was heavy for her, and sometimes she needed help.

Carole Hanson came over to give her a hand.

"Thanks, Carole," Max said. "The Saddle Club team did well today, too. But maybe these girls showed even The Saddle Club a thing or two."

"You could be right about that," Carole told him. "The junior team won the games for Pine Hollow today."

At that, May, Jasmine, and Corey exchanged another high five.

18 Best Friends

Inside her stable at home, Jasmine finished grooming and feeding Outlaw. She was still feeling wonderful from the good job they'd done against Cross County, even if it meant beating Joey Dutton. Now she wanted to be with her teammates. She walked over to Corey's backyard and poked her head into the barn.

"You there?" she called into the stable.

"Yes. I'm just giving Sam some extra carrots," Corey said.

Jasmine laughed. "I gave Outlaw three."

May walked in the door of Corey's stable then. "I brought Samurai some carrots," she announced. Then she saw Jasmine there. "I have some for Outlaw, too," she said.

This time Corey laughed. "Three great

minds thinking exactly the same thing at the same time."

"Aaah-oooooooooow!"

May and Jasmine looked at one another. It was *the* sound.

Corey grinned. "*Some* people might think that was coming from a monster," she said. "But it's only a dog. Would you like to meet Dracula?"

"Dracula?" asked May. "That's his name?"

Corey shrugged. "What else do you name a dog who howls like that?

"Here, boy!" she called. Dracula raced into the stable from outside. He was a big black dog. His tail wagged wildly. The minute he saw Corey, he jumped up on her and began smothering her with kisses.

"He wouldn't hurt a flea!" cried Jasmine.

Just for that, Dracula started licking Jasmine, too. She giggled when his wet tongue tickled her.

Then came the sound of a car's brakes screeching.

May's eyes opened wide. There was *that* sound again! Both she and Jasmine looked to Corey.

"That's Bluebeard—our parrot. He knows

how to make the weirdest sounds. He cackles like a witch and he does tires screeching."

Then there was a whimpering sound. It came from behind the stable. May and Jasmine looked at one another. What now?

"Come see this, but be quiet, okay?" Corey said.

"Okay," the girls agreed. They tiptoed out back. There was a large box there and in it was a golden retriever. She wasn't alone, though. She was completely surrounded by tiny puppies.

"Oh!" Jasmine cried.

"They're so cute!" said May.

"They were born last week," said Corey. "Mom has to come out here every couple of hours to check on them. It's a lot of work."

"I bet it is," said May. She remembered the lights that went on inside the house at night.

Jasmine thought about the person in a long robe who had walked from the house to the stable. There were no more mysteries. There were no monsters. There was no mad scientist. There was just Corey and now she was their friend. The best part was, Jasmine had a feeling she was going to be a really good friend.

Pony Crazy

"You know, I've been thinking," May spoke up.

"Uh-oh," said Jasmine. "What is it this time?"

May shook her head. "It's not a crazy idea, I promise. I've just been thinking about us. You know how The Saddle Club is the head of Horse Wise?"

Jasmine nodded. "They're all really good riders."

"Aren't they older than we are?" Corey asked.

"That's the point," said May. "If they're the head, then what does that make us?"

"The tail?" Corey suggested.

"Right!" May grinned.

Then all three of them said exactly the same thing at exactly the same time: "We're The Pony Tails!"

"That's the only way to describe three pony-crazy girls like us!" Jasmine exclaimed.

Once again the three Pony Tails were thinking the same thing at the same time. This time it was how happy they were to be with their best friends.

MAY'S PONY GROOMING TIPS

My dad taught me that horseback riding isn't only about climbing a horse or pony's saddle. Being a good rider involves taking care of my pony, too. That means feeding Macaroni, making sure he sees the vet regularly, and grooming him every time I ride. This is how I do Macaroni's regular grooming.

I keep all my grooming tools and brushes in a bucket. The first step in grooming a pony is using a tool called a hoofpick. That's what you need to clean out a pony's hooves. I do Macaroni's left front foot first, then left hind, then right front and right hind. If I always do it in the same order, I don't get mixed up and Macaroni gets used to it, too. When you're

picking up a pony's foot, you have to run your hand down his leg so you don't surprise him. Dad showed me how to use the hoofpick so it gets all the dirt and stones out of Macaroni's hooves and doesn't hurt him.

Macaroni's coat is a light color so I always need to give him a sponge bath. If he's really dirty, he gets a shower, too, but most of the time a sponge and a special pony shampoo do the trick.

After the sponge bath comes the curry-comb. I put the currycomb in my right hand and start at the top of his neck. I rub in a cir-cular motion. That loosens dirt and shedded hair. When the currycomb gets dirty, I clean it with another brush called a dandy brush and get back to work. First I do his left side, then his right. I don't use the comb on his face or lower legs. It's too harsh for those areas. I

would never do anything that would hurt Macaroni.

Next comes the stiff dandy brush. It removes the dirt and hair that the comb loosened. I can use it on Macaroni's legs because it doesn't hurt. I also use that to brush Macaroni's mane and tail.

Then comes the soft dandy brush. I use two at a time, one on each hand. They smooth Macaroni's hair back down. Then I take a small sponge and clean his face. I have to be very careful there—especially around his eyes. He's a good pony, though, and he stands completely still for me. I am so lucky!

If I'm getting Macaroni ready for a show or another special event, I'll do some more grooming, like braiding his mane and putting polish on his hooves. But usually the last step

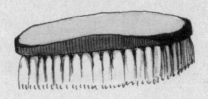

is rubbing him all over with a towel until his coat gets neat and shiny.

Macaroni loves to be brushed and combed and I like to do it. I always feel proud of how handsome my pony looks!

About the Author

Bonnie Bryant was born and raised in New York City, and she still lives there today. She spends her summers in a house by a lake in Massachusetts.

Ms. Bryant began writing about girls and horses when she started *The Saddle Club* in 1987. So far there are more than fifty books in that series! Much as she liked telling the stories about Stevie, Carole, and Lisa, she found that the younger riders at Pine Hollow, notably May Grover, seemed to have stories of their own that needed telling. That's how *Pony Tails* was born.

Ms. Bryant rides horses when she has time away from her computer, but she doesn't have a horse of her own. She likes to ride different horses, enjoying a variety of riding experiences. She thinks most of her readers are much better riders than she is!